Lily the L

Lily's brown pointed ears twitched as she listened to the doors of Mrs Harper's red car slamming shut. The engine started up and the car pulled slowly away, following the rumbling removals lorry.

The sound of the engine slowly faded away, then disappeared completely. Lily was alone.

Titles in Jenny Dale's PUPPY TALES™ series

Coming Next

More of Jenny Dale's PUPPY TALES
stories follow soon

All of Jenny Dale's PUPPY TALES books can
be ordered at your local bookshop or are
available by post from Book Service by Post
(tel: 01624 675137)

Lily the Lost Puppy

by Jenny Dale

Illustrated by Frank Rodgers

A Working Partners Book

MACMILLAN CHILDREN'S BOOKS

For Isabel, Peter and Jessie
Special thanks to Lucy Raby

First published 1999 by Macmillan Children's Books
a division of Macmillan Publishers Limited
25 Eccleston Place, London SW1W 9NF
Basingstoke and Oxford

Associated companies throughout the world

Created by Working Partners Limited
London W12 7QY

ISBN 0 330 37360 9

5 7 9 8 6

A CIP catalogue record for this book is available from
the British Library.

Typeset by Macmillan Children's Books
Printed by Mackays of Chatham plc, Kent

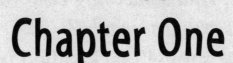

Chapter One

"Lily! Watch out!" Jack was dragging an empty suitcase across his bedroom floor, right over where Lily was sniffing a really interesting patch of bare floorboard. It was full of new smells because the carpet had been taken up only the day before.

Hmm, thought Lily, as her small black nose snuffled along the floor. *Just the faintest whiff of mouse. And something else – old biscuit crumbs, maybe?*

"Lily, move!" Jack called out again.

"OK, OK! Keep your hair on!" Lily yapped crossly as she skipped out of the way. Wherever she was, Lily seemed to be in the wrong place at the moment.

During the last few days, the whole family seemed to have gone mad! There were boxes all over the house and everyone was making a huge fuss about packing things into them. Even Jack had been behaving oddly – he'd hardly played with her for ages. And he was supposed to be her best mate!

Lily lay down with her head between her paws. Why was everyone packing their things away? Was it some sort of game? No, it couldn't be, because when she'd started playing in all that lovely newspaper lying on the hall floor yesterday, she'd got into trouble.

Jack packed the last of his clothes into a suitcase and tried to shut the lid. He'd put far too many things in it. Lily watched as Jack bounced up and down on the suitcase, trying to get the two edges to meet. After a lot of hard work, he managed to get the lid closed at last and clicked the two clasps together.

"*Now* can we play?" yapped Lily, sitting up and cocking her head to one side.

"OK, Lil, we'll go and play in a minute," Jack replied. "I've just got one more thing to do first."

Lily slumped back down again, then spotted a shoelace hanging out of the suitcase. She trotted over and sniffed it. *Brilliant!* she thought. *I'd know that shoelace anywhere. It belongs to one of the trainers Jack uses for football.* She grabbed the shoelace and started tugging.

"Hey, stop it, Lil!" cried Jack.

But Lily carried on. She tugged and tugged, and suddenly the lid of the suitcase burst open. Lily yipped in delight. This was more like it! She picked up the trainer in her teeth and shook it playfully.

"Drop it, Lily!" said Jack sternly. "That's one of my best trainers."

"No way," growled Lily. "It's one of your smelliest."

Jack made a grab for the trainer, but Lily held on, and won. She raced out of the bedroom and downstairs, with the trainer still clamped firmly in her mouth. Jack clattered down after her.

As they raced along the hall, Mr Harper, Jack's father, came out of the living room. "I hope you've finished your packing, Jack," he called. "The removals men will be here any minute."

Lily skidded across the kitchen floor and made for the dog flap in the back door. But the square hole of the dog flap wasn't wide enough for Lily *and* Jack's trainer. Lily bounced back and landed in a heap.

"Aha! Gotcha!" cried Jack, as he caught up with Lily and grabbed the trainer away from her. She then shot through the dog flap and into the back

garden. Jack opened the door
and raced after her.

They followed their usual
marathon route across the small
lawn: round the fishpond – twice
both ways, round the birch tree,
across to the vegetable patch and
back down the other side . . .
Then Lily stopped in her tracks as
she heard a deep rumbling sound
outside in the street.

"That's the lorry coming to take everything away!" cried Jack.

"What?" yelped Lily. She cocked her head at Jack. "Why would they want to do that?"

"Come on, Lil, we're moving to a new house," Jack explained. "It's got a huge garden. We'll have a great time there!"

Lily went cold all over. Her stumpy little tail went right down, in protest. "But I don't want to go!" she growled. "I like it here!"

Jack took no notice and raced back to the house. Lily followed, feeling very upset. She didn't want to move to a strange new house. She had friends round here. There was Bruce the Labrador at Number 10. And Wendy the Sheltie, who lived round the corner. They met every day in the park. Lily hadn't even said goodbye to them!

The house was now full of men in overalls, clumping all over the place. They were shouting to each other in loud voices and carrying all the furniture out of the house. Mrs Harper, Jack's mum, was fussing round, telling them to be careful.

Lily peered out of the front door and watched the men putting furniture into the huge lorry which was waiting outside in the road with its back doors open. It was all too much for Lily. She started shivering in fright.

Jack noticed and held out his arms. "Here, Lil!" he called. She leapt gratefully into his arms and snuggled against his chest.

"Exciting, isn't it?" said Jack, ruffling the wiry white fur at Lily's neck.

Lily watched as the kitchen table was carried through the front door. "*I* don't think so!" she whined back. "I think it's *scary*!"

Chapter Two

When all the rolled-up carpets
and furniture had gone, the men
started to carry boxes outside to
the lorry. Mr Harper came out of
the kitchen with Lily's basket.
"Perhaps Lily should come
with me," he told Jack's mum.
"There's more room in my car

for her basket." He started taking it outside.

"Hey! Where are you going with that?" barked Lily.

"Don't worry, Lily, all your toys are in there!" said Mr Harper, smiling as he walked towards the front door. "Come on then!" he called to her, over his shoulder.

Jack put Lily down. "Go with Dad, Lil," he said. "I'm just going to say goodbye to my bedroom."

Lily hesitated – she'd much rather stay with Jack – then trotted outside after Mr Harper. He put her basket on the back seat of his large car which was parked in front of Mrs Harper's smaller red one, then nodded towards the open car door. "In you go then, Lily," he said.

Lily jumped in reluctantly and Mr Harper slammed the door shut. Lily circled round in her basket a few times, nudging the blanket around to get her bed how she liked it. Just then, there was a loud crunch as one of the men hit something hard against the lorry door.

"Hey! Careful with that!" Mr Harper called out, and went over to see if anything had been damaged.

Lily whined unhappily. She hated being on her own, and everything was suddenly so strange and frightening. She wanted to be with Jack.

Then Lily noticed that one of the

front doors of the car wasn't quite shut. She leapt out of her basket, over into the front seat and slipped out through the gap.

Back in the house, Jack was nowhere to be seen. *Maybe he's still in his bedroom*, Lily thought. She trotted upstairs, her claws clicking on the bare wooden floorboards. But there was no sign of him.

Lily hung around, having a few final sniffs in the corners of the room before continuing her search.

Then suddenly, something terrible happened. Jack's bedroom door slammed shut. Someone had shut Lily in!

Lily was so surprised she didn't do anything at first. She heard someone shutting the other bedroom doors, and the heavy front door slammed shut. Then the roaring engine of the lorry started up. She couldn't believe it. Surely they weren't going without her?

Lily rushed over and scratched furiously at the bottom of the bedroom door, but it was shut tight. She leapt up at the door handle and caught at it with her paw, but the door stayed shut. She began to bark and bark like mad, but the lorry was making so much noise outside, nobody could hear her.

Lily heard Mr Harper's car engine start up. She ran over to the window. But even when she stood up on her hind legs, she was too short to reach the windowsill.

"See you there!" she heard Mr Harper shout out as the lorry doors clanged shut.

"OK!" Mrs Harper shouted back. Lily heard his car slowly driving away.

Very faintly, over the noise of

the lorry, Jack's voice came floating up to Lily. "Lily did go with Dad, didn't she?"

Lily's ears pricked up. "No, I didn't!" she barked. "I'm here!" She scrabbled a bit more under the windowsill, trying desperately to reach it.

"Yes, I saw her get in the car," Lily heard Jack's mum reply. "She'll be there, waiting for you at the new house."

Lily's heart pounded with fear and panic, thumping painfully against her chest. "No!" she barked. "Don't go without me!"

"Hey!" she heard Jack say. "That sounded a bit like Lily!"

"It can't be," his mum replied. "She's gone with Dad. I told you – I saw her get in the car."

Lily took a deep breath and leapt as high as she could, above the windowsill, hoping that Jack would see her. But she couldn't stay up in the air, and he didn't look up at the right time.

Lily's brown pointed ears twitched as she listened to the doors of Mrs Harper's red car

slamming shut. The engine started up and the car pulled slowly away, following the rumbling removals lorry. Lily heard it make the crunching noise it always made when it was going round corners. It must be turning into the avenue where she and Jack walked to the park.

The sound of the engine slowly faded away, then disappeared completely. Lily was alone.

Lily stayed at the window for a while, listening for the sound of the car to return. Surely they would come back for her? But the street remained silent. She began to whimper. Her white furry body quivered with shock.

Then, suddenly, a little spark of courage lit up inside her. "Come on! Be brave!" she told herself.

She stood up and shook herself, then circled the room trying to think what to do next.

She looked at the door. Maybe, if she tried really hard, she could jump up high enough to reach the door handle with her paw. Then she could get out of the house, run down the street and catch up with Jack.

Yes!

Lily went over and started to leap up at the door handle. At first she kept missing. But she kept on, jumping again and again on her short, strong legs. At last, she caught the handle with her

front paws. It jerked down as Lily
fell back, and the catch gave way.
The door swung open. She'd
done it!

Lily pushed the door further
open with her nose. In a flash,
she was out of the room and
streaking down the stairs. She
skidded across the bare floorboards of the hallway towards
the kitchen and . . .

. . . slammed straight into the
closed kitchen door. For the
second time that day, Lily landed
in a heap. The door was shut tight,
and the handle was much higher
than the one in Jack's bedroom.

Lily would never be able to
reach it. All was lost!

She slumped miserably against

the door and let out a howl of despair.

Then Lily heard the sound of a car engine outside. Doors slammed. She heard voices and footsteps coming up the front path. Jack had missed her after all, and had come back for her.

Hurrah!

Lily ran to the front door, her little stump of a tail wagging so hard she thought it would fall off.

She heard the rattle of keys. "Woof!" she barked happily. "I'm still here!"

"What was that?" said a woman's voice.

"What does Mrs Harper mean?" wondered Lily. "Surely she knows it's me!"

The keys rattled a bit more, then the front door swung open. But the people standing in the doorway weren't Lily's family.

Chapter Three

"Goodness!" said the lady who wasn't Mrs Harper. "What are *you* doing here?"

Lily's heart sank as she looked up at the strangers. "What are *you* doing here?" she barked. "I wanted it to be Jack!" Lily's mind raced. She didn't want to stay here! There was only one thing to do.

Lily shot out of the front door past the strange family, down the path and out of the gate. She ran down the street, heading in the direction in which she'd heard Mrs Harper's red car going.

"Hey! Where are you going?" barked Bruce through the gate at Number 10.

"Sorry, can't stop!" woofed Lily breathlessly over her shoulder. "I've got to find Jack!"

Lily raced round the corner into the road lined with trees. She knew it like the back of her paw – it led to the big noisy road at the end, with the park on the other side, where she and Jack went for walks. Without even stopping to sniff at lamp-posts she ran on, with the wind rushing past her ears.

At the corner Lily skidded to a halt. How would she know which way the red car had turned next? She growled in despair, looking up and down the road.

In the doorway of the corner shop she spotted Yeoman, the old sheepdog who lived there. *He might have seen which way the car went*, thought Lily. She trotted eagerly up to him.

"What are you doing out on your own, Lily?" he asked.

"Something terrible has happened," she whined. "My family have gone to live

somewhere else and left me
behind by mistake!"

"Oh dear," Yeoman replied.
"Don't you think you'd better go
back and wait for them? They're
bound to come back for you."

"*No!*" yelped Lily. "Some
strange people have arrived at
the house!" She asked Yeoman if
he'd seen Mrs Harper's red car,
but he hadn't.

"But Wendy might have seen the car," Yeoman suggested. "She sees everything in this street! She's just gone off to the park with her owner."

"I'd better go and find her," Lily said. She trotted briskly to the main road.

A loud motorbike sped past, making Lily jump. Her brown eyes opened wide with fright. She cowered on the pavement for a while. The traffic seemed even noisier and faster than usual. She'd never tried to cross a road on her own before. If only she was here with Jack, and on her lead.

Then Lily noticed the black and white stripes on the road, where she and Jack usually crossed. The traffic had stopped there and people were walking across, so Lily followed, lost amongst a sea of legs.

As soon as she reached the other side, Lily darted through the park gates. She looked round, searching for Wendy, but there was no sign of her.

Lily trotted over to the pond, where she and Jack used to have such fun feeding the ducks. Her tail drooped sadly. "Oh, where *is* he?" she howled.

At that moment, Jack was slumped miserably on the stairs at the new house. "I *did* hear Lily barking in the old house!" he wailed at his parents. "And now she's run off and I might never see her again!" His shoulders heaved with sobs.

The Harpers had arrived at the new house and discovered the terrible mistake. Mr Harper had thought Lily was still in his car when he'd driven off. After all, he hadn't seen her get out. But when Mrs Harper phoned the old house, the new family had told her they'd seen Lily – and she'd run off!

"We must go and look for her, straight away!" Jack cried.

"OK," his mum agreed. "Let's go. Dad can stay here and start the unpacking."

*

Back in the park, Lily sat by the pond, her small body shivering, despite the sunshine.

"Hey! What's the matter?"

Lily looked up. It was Wendy, the Sheltie, coming towards her, wagging her long feathery tail. Wendy's owner was sitting on a bench nearby.

"What are you doing out here on your own?" Wendy asked.

Lily told her the whole sad story and asked if Wendy had seen Jack go past in his mum's red car.

Wendy put her head on one side and thought hard. "Well," she began slowly, "there are quite a lot of red cars around . . . but wait a minute!" She yelped excitedly. "Yes, I do remember! It turned

into the main road, and went –
that way!" Wendy turned her
head to point out the direction.
"But I'd take the short cut
through the park, if I were you,"
she advised wisely. "Better than
going back onto that busy main
road."

"Thanks, Wendy!" said Lily
gratefully and ran off in the
direction Wendy had pointed.

Lily ran and ran, coming to a
side of the park that she and Jack
had never been to. She slowed
down and looked around, panting.

It was all very different here.
The shops outside the railings
seemed smarter, and the houses
and gardens were bigger.

Lily was very thirsty. She

found a small puddle and drank greedily from it. *Yuk!* It tasted horrible. She spat it out again.

"These dogs from the other side of the park have such dreadful manners!"

Lily turned round and saw two large, snooty-looking dogs with lots of silky hair that fell around them like curtains. They were pulling their owner along on two long stretchy leads. They came towards Lily and began sniffing her in a most unfriendly way. Lily noticed they had very smart collars on.

"Oh dear, what kind of scruffy pup is this?" said one.

"And what kind of owner lets such a youngster run loose in the park?" sniffed the other. "Honestly! Some humans!"

The two tall dogs towered over Lily, looking down their long thin noses at her.

Lily's legs stiffened and the wiry hair on her back bristled angrily. They were being rude about Jack! She was about to tell the snooty dogs just what she thought of them when a familiar noise made

Lily prick up her ears. It was the crunching sound of Mrs Harper's car engine.

"Excuse me!" she barked, and ran out from behind the two dogs – just in time to see Jack's mum's red car driving past.

Lily yelped with excitement and dashed out through the park gates after the car. She raced down the pavement, dodging people's legs. She just had to catch up with it! Without looking, she galloped out onto the road – then heard a roaring sound, getting louder and louder – and nearer. Lily looked up and saw a big red bus coming towards her!

Chapter Four

Lily cowered, frozen in terror. Then she realised that the bus had slowed down. Luckily for Lily it was stopping to let passengers on and off.

Lily crept back onto the pavement and watched as the bus slowly pulled away again.

There was no sign of the red car now. She whined miserably.

Suddenly a strange rumbling noise came from Lily's tummy. She realised she was very hungry! *I might as well go and find something to eat*, she thought.

With a heavy heart, Lily got up and trotted off down the street, sniffing the air for smells of food.

A couple of streets away, Jack and his mum had stopped the car to talk to a lady who was being dragged along by the two snooty dogs who'd been rude to Lily.

"Have you seen a Jack Russell puppy who looks lost?" Jack asked.

The lady thought for a moment,

then smiled. "Yes," she replied. "Not long ago, in the park. Perdita and Polly went up to her, then she ran out through the park gates."

"It must have been Lily!" cried Jack excitedly.

"Did you see which direction she went?" Mrs Harper asked.

The lady shook her head.

Jack's shoulders drooped. "She could have gone anywhere!" he said miserably.

Jack's mum thanked the lady and turned to comfort him. "We'll just keep on looking," she said. "Lily can't be very far away!"

Lily wandered further and further in her search for food. She didn't recognise this street at all.

She passed a house with a delicious smell of cooking coming from it and pushed her nose through the gate.

"Rarrghhh! Rarrrghhh!"

Lily leapt backwards in fright as a huge pair of snarling jaws appeared from nowhere. They belonged to an enormous black dog who loomed above her in a very scary way.

"Scram, pup! This is my patch!" he snapped.

Lily didn't hang about. She turned tail, running and running, until she came to an alleyway lined with dustbins and big black bags. Food!

She started nosing around the bags. When she found one that

smelled promising, she tore it open with her sharp white teeth.

Inside, she found a stale crust of bread and the remains of a hamburger, which she gulped down hungrily.

"You can tell this one hasn't been on the streets for long!"

Lily turned to see a pair of scruffy mongrels staring at her. They looked a bit rough, but they were wagging their tails in a friendly way.

"Oh, pardon me," woofed Lily politely. "Is this your patch?"

The two mongrels wagged their tails harder. "We don't believe in that sort of thing," said one. "We strays range far and wide! We hunt in groups and share everything."

"So what's your story, little one?" asked the other stray. "Have you been away from home long?"

Lily poured out the whole sorry story. The two mongrels listened, cocking their heads sympathetically.

"Don't worry," said one of them, when she'd finished. "You're not alone any more. My name's Sam and this is Shep. We'll look after you. Come with us and we'll find you a delicious meal!"

Lily followed her two new friends through a maze of narrow side streets and alleyways until they came to a courtyard full of dustbins. They smelled strongly of all sorts of delicious food.

"Here we are!" announced Sam proudly. "The back of Marcello's restaurant. Best nosh in town!"

In no time, Sam and Shep had raided the dustbins and brought out a variety of tasty leftovers. There was steak and chicken, with crunchy biscuits for afters. They all tucked in greedily.

"Well!" woofed Sam, when they'd all had their fill. "I think

it's time to visit the dump and
see if we can find anything
interesting to chew on. It's a great
way to round off a good meal!
Coming, Lily?"

"Well, I'd like to," replied Lily
politely, "but I really must keep
on looking for Jack."

The other two dogs looked
disappointed. "Aren't you going
to join our gang?" asked Shep.

"If you don't mind, I'd rather
not," said Lily. "But I'm very
grateful to you both. I'll never
forget your kindness."

Sam cocked his head at her. "It's
a great life on the streets, you
know. Freedom, independence,
adventure . . ."

"But I want to be with Jack," Lily

explained. "He means more to me than anything in the world."

Lily trotted on until she came to a neighbourhood on the edge of town with wide, tree-lined roads. The houses were bigger than the one she had lived in with Jack. They had bigger gardens too. Lily could see fields and woods in the distance. But she was exhausted and sat down to rest.

"Oh, look at that little puppy. She must be lost!"

Lily looked up and saw a girl about the same age as Jack, with her parents.

The girl came towards Lily and held her hand out. "Come here, puppy," she coaxed.

Lily shrank away at first but she was too tired to run any more, and these people looked very kind and nice. They reminded Lily of her own family. She let her tail give a tiny wag.

"What shall we do with her?" said the girl's mother. She picked Lily up and inspected her collar. "There's no name tag or telephone number," she said.

"Can we keep her?" asked the girl excitedly.

"No, Sally," said her father. "She must belong to someone. We'd better take her to the Dogs' Home. They'll look after her till her owners come and get her."

Lily found herself being carried into the driveway of a nearby house and placed on Sally's lap in the back seat of a big yellow car.

Sally began to stroke Lily, slow soothing strokes along her furry head and back. Lily began to feel sleepy. She gave Sally's hand a lick then curled up, ready to have a snooze.

The car engine started up. Then suddenly, as the car pulled out of the driveway, Lily heard a familiar sound. It was the crunching noise of Mrs Harper's car engine, coming round the corner.

Lily's ears pricked and she sat up, wide awake again. She jumped off Sally's lap and stood up on her hind legs to peer out of the back window.

There were Jack and his mum in

the red car! Jack's face was
streaming with tears. They were
pulling into the driveway next
door!

Lily started to bark, but Jack
couldn't hear her. The yellow car
was gathering speed now, taking
her further and further away. She
whined, then started to howl at
the top of her voice.

"It's all right, puppy," said Sally, stroking Lily again. "Calm down. You needn't be frightened of the car."

"I'm not!" Lily barked back. "You don't understand! I've finally found Jack and now you're taking me away from him!"

Chapter Five

The blanket in Lily's cage at the Dogs' Home smelled funny, like the stuff Jack's mum used to clean the kitchen. Lily circled round on the blanket a few times, then settled down. She was in a large, bright room full of other cages.

Lily had never seen so many dogs in her life. There were all sorts of colours, shapes and sizes, barking and whining in different voices. They had all looked up when she'd been brought in, then carried on making their din.

Lily's heart felt sad and heavy. What if Jack didn't come to find her? She'd never see him again! She sighed and settled down into a fretful sleep.

"Oh, Mrs Boyd, why did you have to leave me on my own!" whined a voice very close by.

Lily opened one eye and peered into the cage next to her. The spaniel sitting there looked very sad. "Hello, I'm Lily," she woofed.

"I'm Charlie," the spaniel replied.

"Who's Mrs Boyd?" Lily asked.

"She was my owner," whimpered Charlie. "We were very happy. But then she was taken to hospital and never came back. Her neighbour brought me here."

Lily's heart went out to Charlie. He was even worse off than her! At least Lily could hope that Jack would come and get her. "Perhaps someone will come along to give you a new home," said Lily kindly.

"No they won't," replied Charlie sadly. "People only want puppies. I'm two years old!"

Lily decided to try and cheer

Charlie up. She started telling him all about her big adventure on the streets, and all the dogs she had met, until his sad, brown eyes began to close in sleep . . .

By morning, the two dogs were firm friends, snuggled up on each side of the cage wall that separated them, fast asleep.

"Here she is! Lily, did you say her name was?"

At the sound of her name, Lily woke with a start and looked up. She blinked and looked again. She couldn't believe her eyes! There, in front of her cage, was Jack! With Mrs Harper, and Sally, the girl who'd brought her here yesterday!

"Lily!" cried Jack. "I'm here! I've come to get you!"

Lily yelped with delight and sat up, wagging her tail so hard it became a blur.

A girl in a green uniform opened the cage and Lily leapt into Jack's arms, licking his face all over. She wriggled so much he nearly dropped her.

Jack was crying and laughing all at the same time, and Mrs

Harper looked a bit tearful too.

"There, Jack! I told you we'd find her!" she said in a rather wobbly voice, dabbing at her eyes with a tissue.

"What an amazing coincidence, Lil!" said Jack. "Somehow you found our new street yesterday. And when Sally and her family came round to welcome us, they told us they'd just taken a lost puppy to the Dogs' Home. It was you!"

Lily licked one of Jack's ears happily. "Yes," she woofed. "Amazing."

"Come on then, Lil! Let's go and show you our new home," said Jack, putting her lead on.

Lily suddenly remembered

Charlie. She looked over Jack's shoulder to say goodbye to him.

"Bye, Charlie!" she barked. "Don't give up hope!"

But Charlie was busy wagging his tail and snuffling away at Sally, who had crouched down beside his cage and was talking to him in a soppy voice.

Once Lily had seen her basket in the kitchen of the new house, the idea of living there didn't seem so strange after all. Jack loved his new bedroom, and Sally had come round to play in their big new garden. She and her family lived next door.

Early one morning, a few days later, Lily was stopped in her tracks as she raced around the garden. She'd heard yapping in Sally's garden. It sounded familiar.

She ran up to a hole in the fence and peered through. Her small black nose touched another, bigger, black nose. Lily recognised it instantly.

"Charlie!" Lily yelped in surprise. "What are you doing in Sally's garden?"

"It's my garden too, now," Charlie woofed happily. "Thanks to you, I've found a new home!"

Charlie explained that when Sally had arrived back from visiting the Dogs' Home, she'd told her mum all about the spaniel she'd made friends with.

She'd persuaded her parents to go and see Charlie. They'd liked him too and had brought him home with them.

"That's great!" yipped Lily happily. "Now *I've* got a friend next door, too!"

"Charlie, come on, let's ask Mum if we can go next door and play with Jack and Lily," said Sally's voice from the other side of the fence.

"See you in a minute," barked Charlie. He turned and ran over to his new owner, his long silky ears flapping.

Lily gave a little leap of joy then trotted off to find Jack. She was bursting with happiness.

Jack came running out to meet

her. "Come on, Lil, race you to the rockery!"

"Wait a minute!" barked Lily, her tail wagging hard. "Our friends are coming round. We can all race together!"